Rooster

Written by Jill Eggleton
Illustrated by Clive Taylor

Maggie had a rooster.
He was a nosey rooster.
He saw her door open. . .

. . .so he went into the house.

20

He looked in bags and boxes.

"**Get out! Get out!**" said Maggie.
"Go and sit on the fence!"

38

One day, the rooster saw
the car door open.
So he got in the car.

He hid under the seat.

Maggie came out.
She put her big shopping bag
in the car.
She didn't see the rooster.

75

Maggie drove off to the city.

The rooster came out
from under the seat.
He looked out the window.

105

He saw people and cars.

He put his head back
and went. . .

Cock-a-doodle-doo!
Cock-a-doodle
doo!

Maggie got a **big** scare.
She stopped the car.

All the cars stopped.

A policeman came up to Maggie.
"You can't stop like that," he said.

"But there's a rooster in my car,"
said Maggie.
"He scared me."

155

The policeman shook his head.
"You can't have a rooster
in the car," he said.
"He will have to come with me."

177

Maggie looked for the rooster.

"He's not here now," she said
to the policeman.

Maggie went home.

She got her bag and went
into her house.
"This bag is very heavy,"
said Maggie.

She put the bag on the floor.
She sat in her chair and
she shut her eyes.

The rooster got out of the bag.

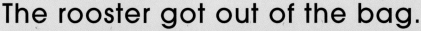

247

When Maggie opened her eyes,
she saw the rooster.
"How did you get home?"
she shouted.

But the rooster just went,
"Cock-a-doodle-doo!" 269

A Route Map

● ● ● ● ●	To the city
▬ ▬ ▬ ▬ ▬	To Maggie's house

Guide Notes

Title: Rooster Trouble

Stage: Early (4) – Green

Genre: Fiction

Approach: Guided Reading

Processes: Thinking Critically, Exploring Language, Processing Information

Written and Visual Focus: Route Map, Thought Bubble

Word Count: 247

THINKING CRITICALLY
(sample questions)
- What do you think this story could be about?
- Focus on the title and discuss.
- Look at pages 2 and 3. What do you think the rooster could have been looking for in Maggie's house?
- Look at page 4. Why do you think the rooster got into the car?
- What do you think might have made the rooster go "Cock-a-doodle-doo!" in the car?
- What do you think the policeman might have done with the rooster?

EXPLORING LANGUAGE

Terminology
Title, cover, illustrations, author, illustrator

Vocabulary
Interest words: trouble, nosey, screech, scare
High-frequency word: there's, gave
Compound words: into, policeman
Positional words: on, under, into, in, cut, up

Print Conventions
Capital letter for sentence beginnings and names (**M**aggie), periods, quotation marks, commas, question mark, ellipsis, exclamation marks